# I Wish I Was Strong Like Manuel

Written by Kathryn Heling and Deborah Hembrook
Illustrated by Bonnie Adamson

*For Troy from your other mom*
*Deborah Hembrook*

*For my dear sister, Amy, always so strong in spirit*
*Kathryn Heling*

*For Mollie–dog*
*Bonnie Adamson*



Heling, Kathryn and Hembrook, Deborah.

I Wish I Was Strong Like Manuel / written by Kathryn Heling and Deborah Hembrook; illustrated by Bonnie Adamson;—1st ed.—Mc Henry, IL : Raven Tree Press, 2009.

p. ; cm

SUMMARY: Willie goes to elaborate and comical lengths to be strong like Manuel. He realizes that he has something that is just as desirable. Willie gains appreciation of his own uniqueness.

English–Only Edition
ISBN: 978-1-934960-52-3 Hardcover
ISBN: 978-1-934960-53-0 Paperback

Bilingual Edition
ISBN: 978-0-9770906-7-9 Hardcover
ISBN: 978-0-9770906-8-6 Paperback

Audience: pre-K to 3rd grade
Title available in English-only or bilingual English-Spanish editions

1. Social Situations / Self-Esteem & Self-Reliance--Juvenile fiction. 2. Social Situations/ Friendshi--Juvenile fiction. 3. Boys and Men--Juvenile fiction. I. Heling, Kathryn and Hembrook, Deborah. II. Adamson, Bonnie, ill. III. Title. IV. Series.

Library of Congress Control Number: 2009921100

Printed in Taiwan
10 9 8 7 6 5 4 3 2
First Edition

**Free activities for this book are available at www.raventreepress.com.**

# I Wish I Was Strong Like Manuel

Written by Kathryn Heling and Deborah Hembrook
Illustrated by Bonnie Adamson

Raven Tree Press
A Division of Delta Systems Co., Inc.
www.raventreepress.com

Hi, my name is Willie.
This is my best friend, Manuel.
I wish I was strong like Manuel.
He looks like a superhero!

Manuel and I go to the gym.
I love using the weights. I feel strong!

I wore my brother's water wings
under my sweater.
They made me look like I had muscles.

BUS

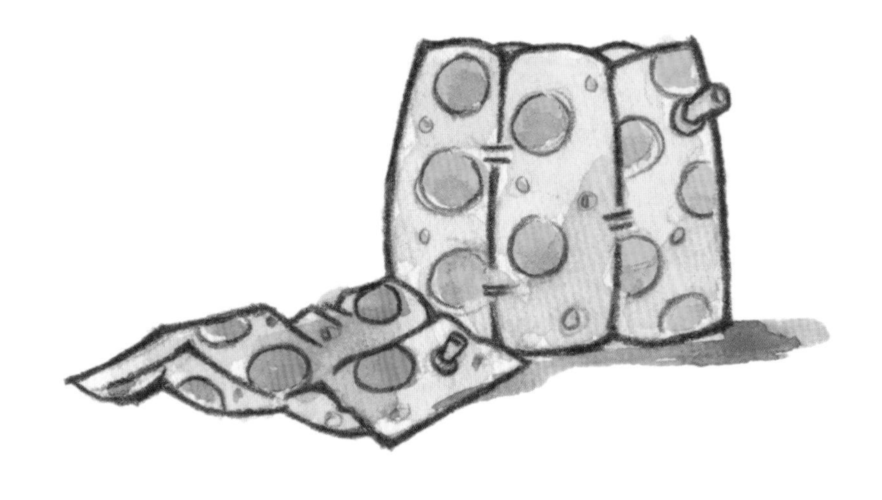

But the air leaked out of one of them.
I'll never do THAT again!

When I play football, I wear shoulder pads.
I pretend they're real muscles.

I wear them all the way home, too!

Mr. Miller needed help.
I said I was strong enough to carry the trash.

What a stinky mess!
I'll never do THAT again!

My dad and I stacked firewood.
I tried to carry the heaviest log.

Ouch!
It fell on my big toe.

I climbed twelve floors to Grandma's apartment.
I thought my legs would get stronger.

But they felt like noodles.
I'll never do THAT again!

I still wish I was
strong like Manuel.

But Manuel wishes
HE was tall like me!

Imagine that!